A Gift for

_____

from

_____

_____

_____ 19____

Dear Parents:

This book was written with the very young child in mind.
It contains some of the most familiar and favorite Mother
Goose rhymes. Along with each rhyme is a fun activity
that gives your child an opportunity to participate. When
you read with your child, encourage him/her to participate
in the rhyme and the activity. The rhymes and the activities
can be read in any order. Young children often like to repeat
the same rhyme over and over again. This book serves
as a good bedtime book. Reading to a child before
bedtime is a good habit to establish with your young child.

We consider books to be life-long gifts that develop and
enhance the love of reading. We hope you enjoy reading
along with Barney!

Mary Ann Dudko, Ph.D.
Margie Larsen, M.Ed.
Early Childhood Educational Specialists

Barney poetry written by Stephen White

Illustrated by Mary Grace Eubank

Book concept by Kathy Parker

Edited by Linda Hartley

Copyright © 1993 by The Lyons Group™
Published by Barney Publishing™ a division of The Lyons Group™

A Division of the Lyons Group

300 East Bethany Dr., Allen, Texas 75002

Barney™ and The Lyons Group™ are the trademarks
of the Lyons Partnership, L.P.

1 2 3 4 5 6 7 8 9 10   96 95 94 93

ISBN 0-7829-0336-3

Library of Congress Catalog Card Number 92-076136

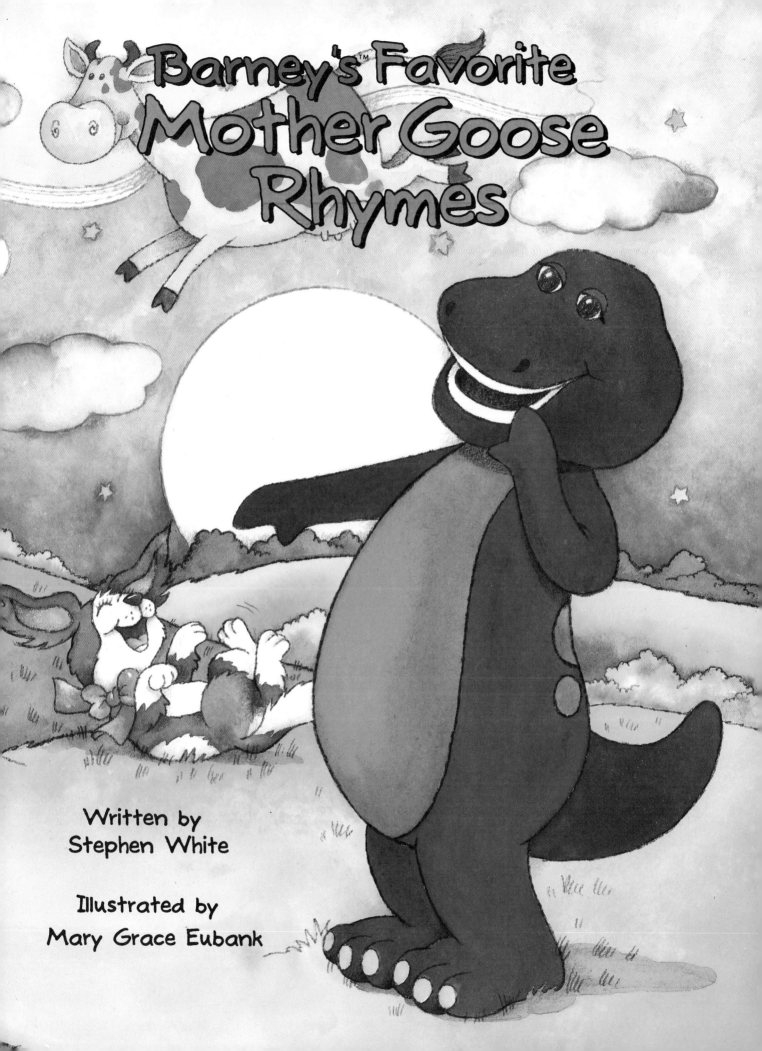

Barney's Favorite Mother Goose Rhymes

Written by
Stephen White

Illustrated by
Mary Grace Eubank

Little Bo Peep

Little Bo Peep has lost her sheep,
And doesn't know where to find them.
Leave them alone, and they'll come home,
Wagging their tails behind them.

Sheep have soft wool —
It makes them feel snug.
Find something soft,
And give it a hug!

Pat-A-Cake

Pat-a-cake, pat-a-cake,
Baker's man!
Bake me a cake as fast as you can.
Pat it and roll it and mark it with "B,"
And put it in the oven for Baby and me.

Barney is playing
The pat-a-cake game —
He's clapping his hands.
Now you do the same!

Little Boy Blue!
Little Boy Blue,
Come blow your horn!
The sheep's in the meadow,
The cow's in the corn.
Where is the little boy
Who looks after the sheep?
He's under the haystack,
Fast asleep.

Let's blow the horn
For Little Boy Blue!
Barney can see it —
Do you see it too?

Humpty Dumpty

Humpty Dumpty sat on a wall,
Humpty Dumpty had a great fall.
All the King's horses,
And all the King's men
Couldn't put Humpty together again.

Wibble, wobble,
and turn around.
Like Humpty Dumpty
we all fall down!

One, Two, Buckle My Shoe

One, two,
Buckle my shoe —
Three, four,
Shut the door —
Five, six,
Pick up sticks —
Seven, eight,
Lay them straight —
Nine, ten,
A big fat hen.

We heard the numbers
From 1 to 10.
Now you and Barney
Can say them again.
1...2...3...4...5...
6...7...8...9...10!

Jack Be Nimble

Jack be nimble,
Jack be quick,
Jack jump over the candlestick.

Barney jumps high
And lands with a thump!
It's your turn to try —
How high can you jump?

To Market

To market, to market, to buy a fat pig,
Home again, home again, jiggety-jig.
To market, to market, to buy a fat hog,
Home again, home again, jiggety-jog.

These little piggies
    make Baby Bop giggle.
Do just like she does,
    and giggle and wiggle!

Ring Around The Rosie
Ring around the rosie,
A pocket full of posies.
Ashes, ashes,
We all fall down!

Barney says, "Reach down and
touch your toes!
Now reach up and touch your nose!"

Two Little Bluebirds
Two little bluebirds sitting on a hill,
One named Jack, and one named Jill.
Fly away, Jack! Fly away, Jill!
Come back, Jack! Come back, Jill!

Barney is making believe
he can fly.
You flap your arms,
and so will I!

Pease Porridge Hot

Pease porridge hot,
Pease porridge cold,
Pease porridge in the pot,
Nine days old.
Some like it hot,
Some like it cold,
Some like it in the pot,
Nine days old.

Barney thinks the porridge
looks yummy —
Pretend you're Barney,
and rub your tummy!

Hey, Diddle Diddle

Hey, diddle, diddle!
The cat and the fiddle,
The cow jumped over the moon.
The little dog laughed
To see such a sport,
And the dish ran away with the spoon.

The cat says, "Meow,"
And the cow says, "Moo, Moo."
Barney says, "Try to make
Sounds like they do."

Wee Willie Winkie

Wee Willie Winkie runs through the town,
Upstairs, downstairs, in his nightgown —
Rapping at the window, crying through the lock,
"Are the children in their beds? For now it's eight o'clock."

Barney likes hearing
the sound of a clock!
Can you help him whisper,
"Tick-tock, tick-tock"?

Twinkle, Twinkle

Twinkle, twinkle, little star,
How I wonder what you are!
Up above the world so high,
Like a diamond in the sky.
Twinkle, twinkle, little star,
How I wonder what you are!

The stars shine so brightly.
The moon's shining too.
Say goodnight to Barney —
He says goodnight to you!

Rock-A-Bye Baby

Rock-a-bye baby
In the tree top,
When the wind blows
The cradle will rock.
When the bough breaks,
The cradle will fall,
And down will come baby,
Cradle and all.

This daddy is singing
some sweet lullabies.
Barney and Baby Bop say,
"Close your eyes."

I Love You

I love you, you love me,
We're a happy family,
With a great big hug,
And a kiss from me to you,
Won't you say
You love me too?

Lyrics by Lee Bernstein
© 1988 The Lyons Group